'OH W
SUCCULENT
BEDROOM!'

CLARICE LISPECTOR
Born 1920, Chechelnik, Ukraine
Died 1977, Rio de Janeiro, Brazil

'Daydreams and Drunkenness of a Young Lady', 'Love' and
'Family Ties' were first published in the short-story collection
Family Ties (Laços de Família) in 1960

CLARICE LISPECTOR

Daydream and Drunkenness of a Young Lady

Translated by Katrina Dodson

PENGUIN BOOKS

PENGUIN CLASSICS

UK | USA | Canada | Ireland | Australia
India | New Zealand | South Africa

Penguin Books is part of the Penguin Random House group
of companies whose addresses can be found at
global.penguinrandomhouse.com.

First published by Penguin Classics 2015
This edition first published 2018
007

Clarice Lispector copyright © Heirs of Clarice Lispector, 1951, 1955,
1960, 1965, 1978, 2010, 2015
Translation copyright © Katrina Dodson, 2015

Set in 12/15 pt Dante MT Std
Typeset by Jouve (UK), Milton Keynes

Printed and bound in Great Britain by Clays Ltd, Elcograf S.p.A.

ISBN: 978-0-241-33760-8

www.greenpenguin.co.uk

Contents

Contents

Daydream and Drunkenness of a Young Lady

('*Devaneio e embriaguez duma rapariga*')

Throughout the room it seemed to her the trams were crossing, making her reflection tremble. She sat combing her hair languorously before the three-way vanity, her white, strong arms bristling in the slight afternoon chill. Her eyes didn't leave themselves, the mirrors vibrated, now dark, now luminous. Outside, from an upper window, a heavy, soft thing fell to the street. Had the little ones and her husband been home, she'd have thought to blame their carelessness. Her eyes never pried themselves from her image, her comb working meditatively, her open robe revealing in the mirrors the intersecting breasts of several young ladies.

'*A Noite!*' called a paperboy into the gentle wind of the Rua do Riachuelo, and something shivered in premonition. She tossed the comb onto the vanity, singing rapturously: 'who saw the lit-tle spar-row . . . go flying past the win-dow . . . it flew so far past Minho!' – but, wrathful, shut herself tight as a fan.

She lay down, fanning herself impatiently with a rustling newspaper in the bedroom. She picked up her handkerchief, breathing it in as she crumpled the coarse embroidery in her reddened fingers. She went back to fanning herself, on the verge of smiling. Oh, dear, she sighed, laughing. She envisioned her bright still-young lady's smile, and smiled even more clos-ing her eyes, fanning herself more deeply still. Oh, dear, came from the street like a butterfly.

'Good day, do you know who came looking for me here at the house?' she thought as a possible and interesting topic of conversation. 'Well I don't know, who?' they asked her with a gallant smile, sorrowful eyes in one of those pale faces that so harm a person. 'Why, Maria Quitéria, man!' she chirped merrily, hands by her side. 'And begging your pardon, who is this young lady?' they persisted gallantly, but now without distinct features. 'You!' she cut off the con-versation with faint resentment, what a bore.

Oh what a succulent bedroom! she was fanning

herself in Brazil. The sun caught in the blinds
quivered on the wall like a Portuguese guitar. The
Rua do Riachuelo rumbled under the panting
weight of the trams coming from the Rua Mem de
Sá. She listened curious and bored to the rattling
of the china cabinet in the parlour. Impatiently,
she turned onto her stomach, and as she lovingly
stretched out her dainty toes, awaited her next
thought with open eyes. 'Finders, seekers,' she
chimed as if it were a popular saying, the kind that
always ended up sounding like some truth. Until she
fell asleep with her mouth open, her drool moisten-
ing the pillow.

She awoke only when her husband came home
from work and entered the bedroom. She didn't
want to have dinner or go out of her way, she fell
back asleep: let the man help himself to the left-
overs from lunch.

And, since the children were at their aunties' farm
in Jacarepaguá, she took the opportunity to wake up
feeling peculiar: murky and light in bed, one of those
moods, who knows. Her husband emerged already
dressed and she didn't even know what the man had
done for breakfast, and didn't even glance at his suit,

whether it needed brushing, little did she care if today was his day to deal with matters downtown. But when he leaned over to kiss her, her lightness crackled like a dry leaf:

'Get away from me!'

'What's the matter with you?' her husband asks astonished, immediately attempting a more effective caress.

Obstinate, she wouldn't know how to answer, so shallow and spoiled was she that she didn't even know where to look for an answer. She lost her temper:

'Oh don't pester me! don't come prowling around like an old rooster!'

He seemed to think better of it and declared:

'Come now, young lady, you're ill.'

She acquiesced, surprised, flattered. All day long she stayed in bed, listening to the house, so silent without the racket from the little ones, without the man who'd have lunch downtown today. All day long she stayed in bed. Her wrath was tenuous, ardent. She only got up to go to the lavatory, whence she returned noble, offended.

The morning became a long, drawn-out afternoon

that became depthless night dawning innocently through the house.

She lay still in bed, peaceful, improvised. She loved . . . In advance she loved the man she'd one day love. Who knows, it sometimes happened, and without guilt or any harm done to either of the two. In bed thinking, thinking, about to laugh as at a bit of gossip. Thinking, thinking. What? well, what did she know. That's how she let herself go on.

From one moment to the next, infuriated, she was on her feet. But in the faintness of that first instant she seemed unhinged and fragile in the bedroom that was spinning, was spinning until she managed to grope her way back to bed, surprised that it might be true: 'come now, woman, let's see if you really are going to get sick!' she said with misgiving. She put her hand to her forehead to see if she'd come down with fever.

That night, until she fell asleep, she fantasticized, fantasticized: for how many minutes? until she passed out: fast asleep, snoring along with her husband.

She awoke behind in the day, the potatoes still to be peeled, the little ones returning from their

aunties' in the afternoon, oh I've even let myself go!,
the day to get the wash done and mend the socks, oh
what a trollop you've turned out to be!, she chided
herself curiously and contentedly, go to the shops,
don't forget the fish, behind in the day, the morning
hectic with sun.

But on Saturday night they went to the tavern in
the Praça Tiradentes at the invitation of that ever-so-
prosperous businessman, she in that new little dress
that while not quite showy was still made of top-
quality fabric, the kind that would last a lifetime.
Saturday night, drunk in the Praça Tiradentes, drunk
but with her husband by her side to vouchsafe her,
and she ceremonious around the other man, so much
classier and wealthier, attempting to engage him in
conversation, since she wasn't just any old village gossip and had once lived in the Capital. But it was
impossible to be more hammered.

And if her husband wasn't drunk, that's because
he didn't want to be disrespectful to the businessman, and, dutifully and humbly, let the other man
rule the roost. Which well suited the classy occasion,
but gave her one of those urges to start laughing!
that scornful mocking! she looked at her husband

stuffed into his new suit and thought him such a joke! It was impossible to be more hammered but without ever losing her ladylike pride. And the *vinho verde* draining from her glass.

And when she was drunk, as during a sumptuous Sunday dinner, all things that by their own natures are separate from each other – scent of olive oil on one side, man on the other, soup tureen on one side, waiter on the other – were peculiarly united by their own natures, and it all amounted to one riotous debauchery, one band of rogues.

And if her eyes were glittering and hard, if her gestures were difficult stages of finally reaching the toothpick dispenser, in fact on the inside she was even feeling quite well, she was that laden cloud gliding along effortlessly. Her swollen lips and white teeth, and the wine puffing her up. And that vanity of being drunk enabling such disdain for everything, making her ripe and round like a big cow.

Naturally she kept up the conversation. For she lacked neither subject nor talent. But the words a person spoke while drunk were like being gravid – words merely in her mouth, which had little to do with the secret center which was like a pregnancy. Oh how peculiar she felt. On Saturday night her everyday soul was lost, and how good it was to lose it, and as a sole memento from those former days her small hands, so mistreated – and here she was now with her elbows on the red-and-white checked tablecloth as if on a card table, profoundly launched into a low and revolutionizing life. And this burst of laughter? that burst of laughter coming mysteriously from her full, white throat, in response to the businessman's finesse, a burst of laughter coming from the depth of that sleep, and the depth of that assurance of one who possesses a body. Her snow-white flesh was sweet as a lobster's, the legs of a live lobster wriggling slowly in the air. And that urge to feel wicked so as to deepen the sweetness into awfulness. And that little wickedness of whoever has a body.

She kept up the conversation, and heard with curiosity what she herself was replying to the wealthy businessman who, with such good timing, had invited them out and paid for their meal. Intrigued and bewildered she heard what she herself was replying: what she said in this condition would be a good omen for the future – already she was no longer a lobster, she was a hard sign: Scorpio. Since she was born in November.

A searchlight as one sleeps that sweeps across the dawn – such was her drunkenness wandering slowly at these heights.

At the same time, what sensibility! but what sensibility! when she looked at that nicely painted picture in the restaurant, she immediately brimmed with artistic sensibility. No one could convince her that she really hadn't been born for other things. She'd always been partial to works of art.

Oh what sensibility! now not only because of the painting of grapes and pears and a dead fish glittering with scales. Her sensibility was uncomfortable without being painful, like a broken nail. And if she wanted she could allow herself the luxury of becoming even more sensitive, she could allow herself the luxury of becoming even more sensitive, she could go further still: because she was protected by a situation, protected like everyone who had attained a position in life. Like someone prevented from a downfall of her own. Oh I'm so unhappy, dear Mother. If she wanted she could pour even more wine into her glass and, protected by the position she'd achieved in life, get even drunker, as long as she didn't lose her pride. And like that, drunker still, she cast her eyes around the restaurant, and oh the scorn for the dull people in the restaurant, not a single man who was a real man, who was truly sad. What scorn for the dull people in the restaurant, whereas she was swollen and heavy, she couldn't possibly be more generous. And everything in the restaurant so remote from each other as if one thing could never speak to another. Each one for himself, and God for all.

Her eyes fixed yet again on that young lady who, from the moment she'd entered, irritated her like mustard in the nose. Right when she'd entered she noticed her sitting at a table with her man, all full of hats and ostentation, blonde like a false coin, all saintly and posh – what a fancy hat she had! – bet she wasn't even married, and flaunting that saintly attitude. And with her fancy hat placed just so. Well let her make the most of that sanctimony! and she'd better not make a mess of that nobility. The most little goody two-shoes were the most depraved. And the waiter, that big dolt, serving her so attentively, the rascal: and the sallow man with her turning a blind eye to it. And that oh-so-holy saint all proud of her hat, all modest with her dainty little waist, bet she couldn't even give him, her man, a son. Oh this had nothing to do with her, honestly: from the moment she'd entered she'd felt the urge to go slap her senseless, right in her saintly blonde girlish face, that little hat-wearing aristocrat. Who didn't even have any curves, who was flat-chested. And bet you that, for all her hats, she was no more than a greengrocer passing herself off as a grande dame.

Oh, how humiliating to have come to the tavern without a hat, her head now felt naked. And that other one with her ladylike airs, pretending to be refined. I know just what you need, you little aristocrat, and your sallow man too! And if you think I'm jealous of you and your flat chest, I'll have you know that I don't give a toss, I don't give a bloody toss about your hats. Lowlife floozies like you, playing hard to get, I'll slap them senseless.

In her sacred wrath, she reached out her hand with difficulty and took a toothpick.

But at last the difficulty of getting home disappeared: she fidgeted now inside the familiar reality of

II

her bedroom, now seated at the edge of her bed with her slipper dangling off her foot.

And, since she'd half-closed her bleary eyes, everything became flesh once more, the foot of the bed made of flesh, the window made of flesh, the suit made of flesh her husband had tossed on the chair, and everything nearly aching. And she, bigger and bigger, reeling, swollen, gigantic. If only she could get closer to herself, she'd see she was bigger still. Each of her arms could be traversed by a person, while unaware it was an arm, and you could dive into each eye and swim without knowing it was an eye. And all around everything aching a little. The things made of flesh had neuralgia. It was the little chill she'd caught while leaving the eatery.

She was sitting on the bed, subdued, skeptical.

And this was nothing yet, God only knew: she was well aware this was nothing yet. That right then things were happening to her that only later would really hurt and matter: once she returned to her normal size, her anaesthetized body would wake up throbbing and she'd pay for all that gorging and wine.

Well, since it'll happen anyway, I may as well open

my eyes now, which she did, and everything became smaller and more distinct, though without any pain at all. Everything, deep down, was the same, just smaller and familiar. She was sitting quite tense on her bed, her stomach so full, absorbed, resigned, with the gentleness of someone waiting for someone else to wake up. 'You overstuff yourself and I end up paying the price,' she said to herself melancholically, gazing at her little white toes. She looked around, patient, obedient. Oh, words, words, bedroom objects lined up in word order, forming those murky, bothersome sentences that whoever can read, shall. Tiresome, tiresome, oh what a bore. What a pain. Oh well, woe is me, God's will be done. What could you do. Oh, I can hardly say what's happening to me. Oh well, God's will be done. And to think she'd had so much fun tonight! and to think it had been so good, and the restaurant so to her liking, sitting elegantly at the table. Table! the world screamed at her. But she didn't even respond, shrugging her shoulders with a pouty tsk-tsk, vexed, don't come pestering me with caresses; disillusioned, resigned, stuffed silly, married, content, the vague nausea.

Right then she went deaf: one of her senses was

missing. She slammed her palm hard against her ear, which only made things worse: for her eardrum filled with the noise of an elevator, life suddenly sonorous and heightened in its slightest movements. It was one or the other: either she was deaf or hearing too much – she reacted to this new proposition with a mischievous and uncomfortable sensation, with a sigh of subdued satiety. To hell with it, she said softly, annihilated.

'And when at the restaurant . . .,' she suddenly recalled. When she'd been at the restaurant her husband's benefactor had slid a foot up against hers under the table, and above the table that face of his. Because it happened to fit or on purpose? That devil. Someone, to be honest, who was really quite interesting. She shrugged.

And when atop her full cleavage – right there in the Praça Tiradentes!, she thought shaking her head incredulously – that fly had landed on her bare skin? Oh how naughty.

Certain things were good because they were almost nauseating: that sound like an elevator in her blood, while her man was snoring beside her, her plump children piled up in the other bedroom asleep, those little scallywags. Oh what's got into me! she thought desperately. Had she eaten too much? oh what's got into me, my goodness!

It was sadness.

Her toes fiddling with her slipper. The not-so-clean floor. How lax and lazy you've turned out. Not tomorrow, because her legs wouldn't be doing so well. But the day after tomorrow just wait and see that house of hers: she'd give it a good scrub with soap and water and scrape off all that grime! just wait and see her house! she threatened wrathfully. Oh she felt so good, so rough, as if she still had milk in her breasts, so strong. When her husband's friend saw her looking so pretty and fat he immediately respected her. And when she began to feel ashamed she didn't know where to look. Oh what sadness. What can you possibly do. Seated at the edge of the bed, blinking in resignation. How well you could see the moon on these summer nights. She leaned forward ever so slightly, indifferent, resigned. The moon. How well you could see it. The high, yellow moon gliding across the sky, poor little thing. Gliding, gliding . . . Up high, up high. The moon. Then the profanity exploded from her in a sudden fit of love: bitch, she said laughing.

Love

('Amor')

A little tired, the groceries stretching out her new knit sack, Ana boarded the tram. She placed the bundle in her lap and the tram began to move. She then settled back in her seat trying to get comfortable, with a half-contented sigh.

Ana's children were good, something true and succulent. They were growing up, taking their baths, demanding for themselves, misbehaved, ever more complete moments. The kitchen was after all spacious, the faulty stove gave off small explosions. The heat was stifling in the apartment they were paying off bit by bit. But the wind whipping the curtains she herself had cut to measure reminded her that if she wanted she could stop and wipe her brow, gazing at the calm horizon. Like a farmhand. She had sown the seeds she had in her hand, no others, but these

alone. And trees were growing. Her brief conversation with the electric bill collector was growing, the
water in the laundry sink was growing, her children
were growing, the table with food was growing, her
husband coming home with the newspapers and
smiling with hunger, the tiresome singing of the
maids in the building. Ana gave to everything, tran-
quilly, her small, strong hand, her stream of life.

A certain hour of the afternoon was more dangerous. A certain hour of the afternoon the trees she
had planted would laugh at her. When nothing else
needed her strength, she got worried. Yet she felt
more solid than ever, her body had filled out a bit
and it was a sight to see her cut the fabric for the
boys' shirts, the large scissors snapping on the cloth.
All her vaguely artistic desire had long since been
directed toward making the days fulfilled and beau-
tiful; over time, her taste for the decorative had
developed and supplanted her inner disorder. She
seemed to have discovered that everything could
be perfected, to each thing she could lend a harmo-
nious appearance; life could be wrought by the hand
of man.

Deep down, Ana had always needed to feel the

firm root of things. And this is what a home bewilderingly had given her. Through winding paths, she had fallen into a woman's fate, with the surprise of fitting into it as if she had invented it. The man she'd married was a real man, the children she'd had were real children. Her former youth seemed as strange to her as one of life's illnesses. She had gradually emerged from it to discover that one could also live without happiness: abolishing it, she had found a legion of people, previously invisible, who lived the way a person works – with persistence, continuity, joy. What had happened to Ana before she had a home was forever out of reach: a restless exaltation so often mistaken for unbearable happiness. In exchange she had created something at last comprehensible, an adult life. That was what she had wanted and chosen.

The only thing she worried about was being careful during that dangerous hour of the afternoon, when the house was empty and needed nothing more from her, the sun high, the family members scattered to their duties. As she looked at the clean furniture, her heart would contract slightly in astonishment. But there was no room in her life for feeling tender toward her astonishment – she'd smother it with the same skill the household chores had given her. Then she'd go do the shopping or get something repaired, caring for her home and family in their absence. When she returned it would be the end of the afternoon and the children home from school needed her. In this way night would fall, with its peaceful vibration. In the morning she'd awake haloed by her calm duties. She'd find the furniture dusty and dirty again, as if repentantly come home. As for herself, she obscurely participated in the gentle black roots of the world. And nourished life anonymously. That was what she had wanted and chosen.

The tram went swaying along the tracks, heading down broad avenues. Soon a more humid breeze blew announcing, more than the end of the afternoon, the end of the unstable hour. Ana breathed deeply and a great acceptance gave her face a womanly air.

The tram would slow, then come to a halt. There was time to relax before Humaitá. That was when she looked at the man standing at the tram stop.

The difference between him and the others was that he really was stopped. Standing there, his hands reaching in front of him. He was blind.

What else could have made Ana sit up warily?
Something uneasy was happening. Then she saw:
the blind man was chewing gum . . . A blind man
was chewing gum.

Ana still had a second to think about how her
brothers were coming for dinner – her heart beat
violently, at intervals. Leaning forward, she stared
intently at the blind man, the way we stare at things
that don't see us. He was chewing gum in the dark.
Without suffering, eyes open. The chewing motion
made it look like he was smiling and then suddenly
not smiling, smiling and not smiling – as if he had
insulted her, Ana stared at him. And whoever saw
her would have the impression of a woman filled
with hatred. But she kept staring at him, leaning further and further forward – the tram suddenly lurched
throwing her unexpectedly backward, the heavy knit
sack tumbled from her lap, crashed to the floor – Ana
screamed, the conductor gave the order to stop
before he knew what was happening – the tram
ground to a halt, the passengers looked around
frightened.

Unable to move to pick up her groceries, Ana
sat up, pale. A facial expression, long unused, had

reemerged with difficulty, still tentative, incomprehensible. The paperboy laughed while returning her bundle. But the eggs had broken inside their newspaper wrapping. Viscous, yellow yolks dripped through the mesh. The blind man had interrupted his chewing and was reaching out his uncertain hands, trying in vain to grasp what was happening. The package of eggs had been thrown from the bag and, amid the passengers' smiles and the conductor's signal, the tram lurched back into motion.

A few seconds later nobody was looking at her. The tram rumbled along the tracks and the blind man chewing gum stayed behind forever. But the damage was done.

The knit mesh was rough between her fingers, not intimate as when she had knit it. The mesh had lost its meaning and being on a tram was a snapped thread; she didn't know what to do with the groceries on her lap. And like a strange song, the world started up again all around. The damage was done. Why? could she have forgotten there were blind people? Compassion was suffocating her, Ana breathed heavily. Even the things that existed before this event were now wary, had a more hostile,

perishable aspect . . . The world had become once
again a distress. Several years were crashing down, the
yellow yolks were running. Expelled from her
own days, she sensed that the people on the street were
in peril, kept afloat on the surface of the darkness by a
minimal balance – and for a moment the lack of meaning left them so free they didn't know where to go. The
perception of an absence of law happened so suddenly
that Ana clutched the seat in front of her, as if she
might fall off the tram, as if things could be reverted
with the same calm they no longer held.

What she called a crisis had finally come. And its
sign was the intense pleasure with which she now
looked at things, suffering in alarm. The heat had
become more stifling, everything had gained strength
and louder voices. On the Rua Voluntários da Pátria
a revolution seemed about to break out, the sewer
grates were dry, the air dusty. A blind man chewing
gum had plunged the world into dark voraciousness.
In every strong person there was an absence of compassion for the blind man and people frightened her
with the vigor they possessed. Next to her was a lady
in blue, with a face. She averted her gaze, quickly.
On the sidewalk, a woman shoved her son! Two

23

lovers interlaced their fingers smiling . . . And the blind man? Ana had fallen into an excruciating benevolence.

She had pacified life so well, taken such care for it not to explode. She had kept it all in serene comprehension, separated each person from the rest, clothes were clearly made to be worn and you could choose the evening movie from the newspaper – everything wrought in such a way that one day followed another. And a blind man chewing gum was shattering it all to pieces. And through this compassion there appeared to Ana a life full of sweet nausea, rising to her mouth.

Only then did she realize she was long past her stop. In her weak state everything was hitting her with a jolt; she left the tram weak in the knees, looked around, clutching the egg-stained mesh. For a moment she couldn't get her bearings. She seemed to have stepped off into the middle of the night.

It was a long street, with high, yellow walls. Her heart pounding with fear, she sought in vain to recognize her surroundings, while the life she had discovered kept pulsating and a warmer, more mysterious wind whirled round her face. She stood there looking at the wall. At last she figured out where she was. Walking a little further along a hedge, she passed through the gates of the Botanical Garden.

She trudged down the central promenade, between the coconut palms. There was no one in the Garden. She put her packages on the ground, sat on a bench along a path and stayed there a long while.

The vastness seemed to calm her, the silence regulated her breathing. She was falling asleep inside herself.

From a distance she saw the avenue of palms where the afternoon was bright and full. But the shade of the branches covered the path.

All around were serene noises, scent of trees, little surprises among the vines. The whole Garden crushed by the ever faster instants of the afternoon. From where did that half-dream come that encircled her? Like a droning of bees and birds. Everything was strange, too gentle, too big.

A light, intimate movement startled her – she spun around. Nothing seemed to have moved. But motionless in the central avenue stood a powerful cat. Its fur was soft. Resuming its silent walk, it disappeared.

Worried, she looked around. The branches were swaying, the shadows wavering on the ground. A sparrow was pecking at the dirt. And suddenly, in distress, she seemed to have fallen into an ambush. There was a secret labor underway in the Garden that she was starting to perceive.

In the trees the fruits were black, sweet like honey. On the ground were dried pits full of circumvolutions, like little rotting brains. The bench was stained with purple juices. With intense gentleness the waters murmured. Clinging to the tree trunk were the luxuriant limbs of a spider. The cruelty of the world was tranquil. The murder was deep. And death was not what we thought.

While imaginary – it was a world to sink one's teeth into, a world of voluminous dahlias and tulips. The trunks were criss-crossed by leafy parasites, their embrace was soft, sticky. Like the revulsion that precedes a surrender – it was fascinating, the woman was nauseated, and it was fascinating.

The trees were laden, the world was so rich it was rotting. When Ana thought how there were children and grown men going hungry, the nausea rose to her throat, as if she were pregnant and abandoned. The moral of the Garden was something else. Now that the blind man had led her to it, she trembled upon the first steps of a sparkling, shadowy world, where giant water lilies floated monstrous. The little flowers scattered through the grass didn't look yellow or rosy to her, but the color of bad gold and scarlet. The decomposition was deep, perfumed . . . But all the heavy things, she saw with her head encircled by a swarm of insects, sent by the most exquisite life in the world. The breeze insinuated itself among the flowers. Ana sensed rather than smelled its sweetish scent . . . The Garden was so pretty that she was afraid of Hell.

It was nearly evening now and everything seemed full, heavy, a squirrel leaped in the shadows. Beneath her feet the earth was soft, Ana inhaled it with delight. It was fascinating, and she felt nauseated.

But when she remembered the children, toward whom she was now guilty, she stood with a cry of pain. She grabbed her bag, went down the dark path, reached the promenade. She was nearly running – and she saw the Garden all around, with its haughty impersonality. She rattled the locked gates, rattled them gripping the rough wood. The guard appeared, shocked not to have seen her.

Until she reached the door of her building, she seemed on the verge of a disaster. She ran to the elevator clutching the mesh sack, her soul pounding in her chest – what was happening? Her compassion for the blind man was as violent as an agony, but the world seemed to be hers, dirty, perishable, hers. She opened her front door. The living room was large, square, the doorknobs were gleaming spotlessly, the window-panes gleaming, the lamp gleaming – what new land was this? And for an instant the wholesome life she had led up till now seemed like a morally insane way to live. The boy who ran to her was a being with long legs and a face just like hers, who ran up and hugged her. She clutched him tightly, in alarm. She protected herself trembling. Because life was in peril. She loved the world, loved what had been created – she loved with nausea. The same way she'd always been fascinated by oysters, with that vaguely sick feeling she always got when nearing the truth, warning her. She embraced her son, nearly to the point of hurting him. As if she had learned of an evil – the blind man or the lovely Botanical Garden? – she clung to him, whom she loved more than anything. She had been touched by the demon of faith. Life is horrible, she said to him softly, ravenous. What would she do if she heeded the call of the blind man? She would go alone . . . There were places poor and rich that needed her. She needed them . . . I'm scared, she said. She felt the child's delicate ribs between her arms, heard his frightened sobbing. Mama, the boy called. She held him away from her, looked at that face, her heart cringed. Don't let Mama forget you, she told him. As soon as the child felt her embrace loosen, he broke free and fled to the bedroom door, looking at her from greater safety. It was the worst look she had ever received. The blood rushed to her face, warming it.

She let herself fall into a chair, her fingers still gripping the mesh sack. What was she ashamed of?

There was no escape. The days she had forged had ruptured the crust and the water was pouring out. She was facing the oyster. And there was no way not to look at it. What was she ashamed of? That it was no longer compassion, it wasn't just compassion: her heart had filled with the worst desire to live.

She no longer knew whether she was on the side of the blind man or the dense plants. The man had gradually receded into the distance and in torture she seemed to have gone over to the side of whoever

had wounded his eyes. The Botanical Garden, tranquil and tall, was revealing this to her. In horror she
was discovering that she belonged to the strong part
of the world – and what name should she give her
violent mercy? She would have to kiss the leper,
since she would never be just his sister. A blind man
led me to the worst in myself, she thought in alarm.
She felt banished because no pauper would drink
water from her ardent hands. Ah! it was easier to be
a saint than a person! By God, hadn't it been real, the
compassion that had fathomed the deepest waters of
her heart? But it was the compassion of a lion.

Humiliated, she knew the blind man would prefer
a poorer love. And, trembling, she also knew why.
The life of the Botanical Garden was calling her as
a werewolf is called by the moonlight. Oh! but
she loved the blind man! she thought with moist
eyes. Yet this wasn't the feeling you'd go to church
with. I'm scared, she said alone in the living room.
She got up and went to the kitchen to help the maid
with dinner.

But life made her shiver, like a chill. She heard the
school bell, distant and constant. The little horror of
the dust threading together the underside of the

oven, where she discovered the little spider. Carrying
the vase to change its water – there was the horror
of the flower surrendering languid and sickening to
her hands. The same secret labor was underway
there in the kitchen. Near the trash can, she crushed
the ant with her foot. The little murder of the ant.
The tiny body trembled. The water droplets were
dripping into the stagnant water in the laundry sink.
The summer beetles. The horror of the inexpressive
beetles. All around was a silent, slow, persistent life.
Horror, horror. She paced back and forth across the
kitchen, slicing the steaks, stirring the sauce. Round
her head, circling, round the light, the mosquitoes of
a sweltering night. A night on which compassion was
raw as bad love. Between her two breasts sweat slid
down. Faith was breaking her, the heat of the stove
stung her eyes.

Then her husband arrived, her brothers and their
wives arrived, her brothers' children arrived.

They ate dinner with all the windows open, on
the ninth floor. An airplane went shuddering past,
threatening in the heat of the sky. Though made with
few eggs, the dinner was good. Her children stayed
up too, playing on the rug with the others. It was

summer, it would be pointless to send them to bed. Ana was a little pale and laughed softly with the others.

After dinner, at last, the first cooler breeze came in through the windows. They sat around the table, the family. Worn out from the day, glad not to disagree, so ready not to find fault. They laughed at everything, with kind and human hearts. The children were growing up admirably around them. And as if it were a butterfly, Ana caught the instant between her fingers before it was never hers again.

Later, when everyone had gone and the children were already in bed, she was a brute woman looking out the window. The city was asleep and hot. Would whatever the blind man had unleashed fit into her days? How many years would it take for her to grow old again? The slightest movement and she'd trample one of the children. But with a lover's mischief, she seemed to accept that out of the flower emerged the mosquito, that the giant water lilies floated on the darkness of the lake. The blind man dangled among the fruits of the Botanical Garden.

If that was the oven exploding, the whole house would already be on fire! she thought rushing into the kitchen and finding her husband in front of the spilled coffee.

'What happened?!' she screamed vibrating all over.

He jumped at his wife's fright. And suddenly laughed in comprehension:

'It was nothing,' he said, 'I'm just clumsy.' He looked tired, bags under his eyes.

But encountering Ana's strange face, he peered at her with greater attention. Then he drew her close, in a swift caress.

'I don't want anything to happen to you, ever!' she said.

'At least let the oven explode at me,' he answered smiling.

She stayed limp in his arms. This afternoon something tranquil had burst, and a humorous, sad tone was hanging over the house. 'Time for bed,' he said, 'it's late.' In a gesture that wasn't his, but that seemed natural, he held his wife's hand, taking her along without looking back, removing her from the danger of living.

The dizziness of benevolence was over.

And, if she had passed through love and its hell,

33

she was now combing her hair before the mirror, for an instant with no world at all in her heart. Before going to bed, as if putting out a candle, she blew out the little flame of the day.

Family Ties
(*'Os laços de família'*)

The woman and her mother finally squeezed into the taxi that was taking them to the station. The mother kept counting and recounting the two suitcases trying to convince herself that both were in the car. The daughter, with her dark eyes, whose slightly cross-eyed quality gave them a constant glimmer of derision and detachment – watched.

'I haven't forgotten anything?' the mother was asking for the third time.

'No, no, you haven't forgotten anything,' the daughter answered in amusement, patiently.

That somewhat comic scene between her mother and her husband still lingered in her mind, when it came time to say goodbye. For the entire two weeks of the old woman's visit, the two could barely stand each other; their good-mornings and good-afternoons constantly struck a note of cautious tact that made her want to laugh. But right when saying goodbye, before getting into the taxi, her mother had transformed into a model mother-in-law and her husband had become the good son-in-law. 'Forgive any misspoken words,' the old lady had said, and Catarina, taking some joy in it, had seen Antônio fumble with the suitcases in his hands, stammering – flustered at being the good son-in-law. 'If I laugh, they'll think I'm mad,' Catarina had thought, frowning. 'Whoever marries off a son loses a son, whoever marries off a daughter gains a son,' her mother had added, and Antônio took advantage of having the flu to cough. Catarina, standing there, had mischievously observed her husband whose self-assurance gave way to a diminutive, dark-haired man, forced to be a son to that tiny graying woman . . . Just then her urge to laugh intensified. Luckily she never actually had to laugh whenever she got the urge: her eyes took on a sly, restrained look, went even more cross-eyed – and her laughter came out through her eyes. Being able to laugh always hurt a little. But she couldn't help it: ever since she was little she'd laughed through her eyes, she'd always been cross-eyed.

'I'll say it again, that boy is too skinny,' her mother

declared while bracing herself against the jolting of the car. And though Antônio wasn't there, she adopted the same combative, accusatory tone she used with him. So much that one night Antônio had lost his temper: 'It's not my fault, Severina!' He called his mother-in-law Severina, since before the wedding he'd envisioned them as a modern mother- and son-in-law. Starting from her mother's first visit to the couple, the word Severina had turned leaden in her husband's mouth, and so, now, the fact that he used her first name hadn't stopped . . . – Catarina would look at them and laugh.

'The boy's always been skinny, Mama,' she replied.

The taxi drove on monotonously.

'Skinny and anxious,' added the old lady decisively.

'Skinny and anxious,' Catarina agreed patiently.

He was an anxious, distracted boy. During his grand-mother's visit he'd become even more remote, slept poorly, was upset by the old woman's excessive affection and loving pinches. Antônio, who'd never been particularly worried about his son's sensitivity, had begun dropping hints to his mother-in-law, 'to protect a child' . . .

'I haven't forgotten anything . . .' her mother started up again, when the car suddenly braked, launching them into each other and sending their suitcases flying. Oh! oh! shouted her mother as if faced with some irremediable disaster, 'oh!' she said shaking her head in surprise, suddenly older and pitiable. And Catarina?

Catarina looked at her mother, and mother looked at daughter, and had some disaster also befallen Catarina? her eyes blinked in surprise, she quickly righted the suitcases and her purse, trying to remedy the catastrophe as fast as possible. Because something had indeed happened, there was no point hiding it: Catarina had been launched into Severina, into a long forgotten bodily intimacy, going back to the age when one has a father and mother. Though they'd never really hugged or kissed. With her father, yes, Catarina had always been more of a friend. Whenever her mother would fill their plates making them overeat, the two would wink at each other conspiratorially and her mother never even noticed. But after colliding in the taxi and after regaining their composure, they had nothing to talk about – why weren't they already at the station?

'I haven't forgotten anything,' her mother asked in a resigned voice.

Catarina no longer wished to look at her or answer.

'Take your gloves!' she said as she picked them up off the ground.

'Oh! oh! my gloves!' her mother exclaimed, flustered.

They only really looked at each other once the suitcases were deposited on the train, after they'd exchanged kisses: her mother's head appeared at the window.

Catarina then saw that her mother had aged and that her eyes were glistening.

The train wasn't leaving and they waited with nothing to say. The mother pulled a mirror from her purse and studied herself in her new hat, bought at the same milliner's where her daughter went. She gazed at herself while making an excessively severe expression that didn't lack in self-admiration. Her daughter watched in amusement. No one but me can love you, thought the woman laughing through her eyes; and the weight of that responsibility left the taste of blood in her mouth. As if 'mother and daughter' were life and abhorrence. No, you couldn't say she loved her mother. Her mother pained her, that was all. The old woman had slipped the mirror back into her purse, and was smiling steadily at her. Her worn and still quite clever face looked like it was struggling to make a certain impression on the people around her, in which her hat played a role. The station bell suddenly rang, there was a general movement of anxiousness, several people broke into a run thinking the train was already leaving: Mama! the woman said. Catarina! the old woman said. They gaped at each other, the suitcase on a porter's head blocked their view and a young man rushing past grabbed Caterina's arm in passing, jerking the collar of her dress off-kilter. When they could see each other again, Catarina was on the verge of asking if she'd forgotten anything . . .

'. . . I haven't forgotten anything?' her mother asked.

Catarina also had the feeling they'd forgotten something, and they looked at each other at a loss – for if they really had forgotten something, it was too late now. A woman dragged a child along, the child wailed, the station bell resounded again . . . Mama, said the woman. What was it they'd forgotten to say to each other? and now it was too late. It struck her that one day they should have said something like: 'I am your mother, Catarina.' And she should have answered: 'And I am your daughter.'

'Don't sit in the draft!' Catarina called.

'Come now, girl, I'm not a child,' said her mother, never taking her attention off her own appearance. Her freckled hand, slightly tremulous, was delicately arranging the brim of her hat and Catarina suddenly wanted to ask whether she'd been happy with her father:

'Give my best to Auntie!' she shouted.

'Yes, of course!'

'Mama,' said Catarina because a lengthy whistle was heard and the wheels were already turning amid the smoke.

'Catarina!' the old woman called, her mouth open and her eyes astonished, and at the first lurch her daughter saw her raise her hands to her hat: it had fallen over her nose, covering everything but her new dentures. The train was already moving and Catarina waved. Her mother's face disappeared for an instant and immediately reappeared hatless, her loosened bun spilling in white locks over her shoulders like the hair of a maiden – her face was downcast and unsmiling, perhaps no longer even seeing her daughter in the distance.

Amid the smoke Catarina began heading back, frowning, with that mischievous look of the cross-eyed. Without her mother's company, she had regained her firm stride: it was easier alone. A few men looked at her, she was sweet, a little heavyset. She walked serenely, dressed in a modern style, her short hair dyed 'mahogany.' And things had worked out in such a way that painful love seemed like happiness to her – everything around her was so alive and tender, the dirty street, the old trams, orange peels – strength flowed back and forth through her heart in weighty abundance. She was very pretty just then, so elegant; in step with her time and the city where she'd been born as if she had chosen it. In her cross-eyed look anyone could sense the enjoyment this woman took in the things of the world. She stared at other people boldly, trying to fasten onto those mutable figures her pleasure that was still damp with tears for her mother. She veered out of the way of oncoming cars, managed to sidestep the line for the bus, glancing around ironically; nothing could stop this little woman whose hips swayed as she walked from climbing one more mysterious step in her days.

The elevator hummed in the beachfront heat. She opened the door to her apartment while using her other hand to free herself of her little hat; she seemed poised to reap the largest of the whole world, the path opened by the mother who was burning in her chest. Antônio barely looked up from his book. Saturday afternoon had always been 'his,' and, as soon as Severina had left, he gladly reclaimed it, seated at his desk.

'Did "she" leave?'

'Yes she did,' answered Catarina while pushing open the door to her son's room. Ah, yes, there was the boy, she thought in sudden relief. Her son. Skinny and anxious. Ever since he could walk he'd been steady on his feet; but nearing the age of four he still spoke as if he didn't know what verbs were: he'd confirm things coldly, not linking them. There he sat fiddling with his wet towel, exact and remote. The woman felt a pleasant warmth and would have liked to capture the boy forever in that moment; she pulled the towel from his hands disapprovingly: that boy! But the boy gazed indifferently into the air, communicating with himself. He was always distracted. No one had ever really managed to hold his attention. His mother shook out the towel and her body blocked the room from his view: 'Mama,'

43

said the boy. Catarina spun around. It was the first time he'd said 'Mama' in that tone of voice and without asking for anything. It had been more than a confirmation: Mama! The woman kept shaking the towel violently and wondered if there was anyone she could tell what happened, but she couldn't think of anyone who'd understand what she couldn't explain. She smoothed the towel vigorously before hanging it to dry. Maybe she could explain, if she changed the way it happened. She'd explain that her son had said: 'Mama, who is God.' No, maybe: 'Mama, boy wants God.' Maybe. The truth would only fit into symbols, they'd only accept it through symbols. Her eyes smiling at her necessary lie, and above all at her own foolishness, fleeing from Severina, the woman unexpectedly laughed aloud at the boy, not just with her eyes: her whole body burst into laughter, a burst casing, and a harshness emerging as hoarseness. Ugly, the boy then said peering at her.

'Let's go for a walk!' she replied blushing and taking him by the hand.

She passed through the living room, informing her husband without breaking stride: 'We're going out!' and slammed the apartment door.

Antônio hardly had time to look up from his book – and in surprise saw that the living room was already empty. Catarina! he called, but he could already hear the sound of the descending elevator. Where did they go? he wondered nervously, coughing and blowing his nose. Because Saturday was his, but he wanted his wife and his son at home while he enjoyed his Saturday. Catarina! he called irritably though he knew she could no longer hear him. He got up, went to the window and a second later spotted his wife and son on the sidewalk.

The pair had stopped, the woman perhaps deciding which way to go. And suddenly marching off.

Why was she walking so briskly, holding the child's hand? through the window he saw his wife gripping the child's hand tightly and walking swiftly, her eyes staring straight ahead; and even without seeing it, the man could tell that her jaw was set. The child, with who-knew-what obscure comprehension, was also staring straight ahead, startled and unsuspecting. Seen from above, the two figures lost their familiar perspective, seemingly flattened to the ground and darkened against the light of the sea. The child's hair was fluttering . . .

The husband repeated his question to himself, which, though cloaked in the innocence of an everyday expression, worried him: where are they going? He nervously watched his wife lead the child and feared that just now when both were beyond his reach she would transmit to their son . . . but what exactly? 'Catarina,' he thought, 'Catarina, this child is still innocent!' Just when does a mother, holding a child tight, impart to him this prison of love that would forever fall heavily on the future man. Later on her son, a man now, alone, would stand before this very window, drumming his fingers against this windowpane; trapped. Forced to answer to a dead person. Who could ever know just when a mother passes this legacy to her son. And with what somber pleasure. Mother and son now understanding each other inside the shared mystery. Afterward no one would know from what black roots a man's freedom is nourished. 'Catarina,' he thought enraged, 'that child is innocent!' Yet they'd disappeared somewhere along the beach. The shared mystery.

'But what about me? what about me?' he asked fearfully. They had gone off alone. And he had stayed behind. 'With his Saturday.' And his flu. In that tidy apartment, where 'everything ran smoothly.' What if his wife was fleeing with their son from that living room with its well-adjusted light, from the tasteful furniture, the curtains and the paintings? That was what he'd given her. An engineer's apartment. And he knew that if his wife enjoyed the situation of having a youthful husband with a promising future – she also disparaged it, with those deceitful eyes, fleeing with their anxious, skinny son. The man got worried. Since he couldn't provide her anything but: more success. And since he knew that she'd help him achieve it and would hate whatever they accomplished. That was how this calm, thirty-two-year-old woman was, who never really spoke, as if she'd been alive forever. Their relationship was so peaceful. Sometimes he tried to humiliate her, he'd barge into their bedroom while she was changing because he knew she detested being seen naked. Why did he need to humiliate her? Yet he was well aware that she would only ever belong to a man as long as she had her pride. But he had grown used to this way of making her feminine: he'd humili-ate her with tenderness, and soon enough she'd smile – without resentment? Maybe this had given rise to the peaceful nature of their relationship, and those muted conversations that created a homey environment for their child. Or would he sometimes get irritable? Sometimes the boy would get irritable, stomping his feet, screaming from nightmares. What had this vibrant little creature been born from, if not from all that he and his wife had cut from their everyday life. They lived so peacefully that, if they brushed up against a moment of joy, they'd exchange rapid, almost ironic, glances, and both would say with their eyes: let's not waste it, let's not use it up frivolously. As if they'd been alive forever.

But he had spotted her from the window, seen her striding swiftly holding hands with their son, and said to himself: she's savoring a moment of joy – alone. He had felt frustrated because for a while now he hadn't been able to live unless with her. And she still managed to savor her moments – alone. For example, what had his wife been up to on the way from the train to the apartment? not that he had any suspicions but he felt uneasy.

The last light of the afternoon was heavy and beat down solemnly on the objects. The dry sands crackled. The whole day had been under this threat of radiating. Which just then, without exploding, nonetheless, grew increasingly deafening and droned on in the building's ceaseless elevator. Whenever Catarina returned they'd have dinner while swatting at the moths. The boy would cry out after first falling asleep, Catarina would interrupt dinner for a moment . . . and wouldn't the elevator let up for even a second?! No, the elevator wouldn't let up for a second.

'After dinner we'll go to the movies,' the man decided. Because after the movies it would be night at last, and this day would shatter with the waves on the crags of Arpoador.